Nene's Prose III

Ancel Mondia

Ukiyoto Publishing

Contents

A View on Manifestation (August 16, 2023)   1

Villain Era (October 13, 2023)   4

Peach Fuzz (December 29, 2023)   8

Thoughts to Ponder: Plan B (March 4, 2024)   13

Puzzle Pieces (August 28, 2024)   18

Inner Speech (November 27, 2024)   23

About the Author   *27*

A View on Manifestation (August 16, 2023)

I recently came across a short video that shows a casual interview with a known songwriter. During the brief talk, he stated that he regrets having composed a song that was about a broken heart.

His regret was caused by an information that his fans, who consider the song as their favorite, had their hearts broken, too. The songwriter believed that the piece he composed affects the psyche and determines life events of its listeners.

The short video reminds me of the concept of manifestation, suggesting that our thinking becomes our prophecies. I became terrified right after I watched the interview because I wasn't really cautious on what songs to listen to.

I also tried to recall my past writings because I was bothered by the idea that I might have impacted my readers' lives in a way that I didn't intend to. I suddenly remembered a friend who asked me about the reason behind the tragic endings of my tales.

She humbly suggested that I could write happy endings instead for positive manifestations as she has been trying to achieve them. I just told her that manifestations were not in the context as I was writing my tales.

To manifest circumstances or consequences is not my purpose, it is instead to bring awareness to possible outcomes when we let our shallow side rule us. It is impossible for us to value positivities when we fail to recognize that negativities exist.

At first, I had doubts about my effect or influence on my readers. But later on, I realized that manifesting negativities was not my purpose, so my tales and other literary pieces can't be considered having the evil eye or black spell.

Then I remembered a poet that told me that what she wrote eventually manifested in her life. Her writings were seemingly a prophecy of her own future, so she suggested that I write only about positive things that I want to happen to me.

I admit I used to believe these views about manifestations, but I began to have my own belief on the matter. I recall that I am a literature major, which points to the reality that I have read multiple literary pieces, but none of them has manifested in my life.

In addition, the stories I have been writing can't be considered as predictions of the future. As far as I remember, none of my writings has happened to me as a circumstance or life event.

My purpose is to deal with past issues and release them through writing. My pieces serve as reminders that the issues shouldn't be done again nor tolerated to recur. My writings primarily are created for awareness.

Additionally, my literary pieces can also be based on present musings, that when being put into writings, can bring entertainment. They help us to make sense through lines and rhymes, that when combined can build scenarios in the mind that show how creativity works.

I admit I have been writing randomly but it doesn't mean that my random works are the cause of my mixed life events. I am sure of my claim because life itself really is a mix of everything if we take it without selection and filters.

Back to that short video of the songwriter, I believe that there is already something in the subconscious of the fans that caused them to be drawn to the song. But it is themselves that manifested their fates, and not the impact of the song nor any other forms of art being created.

Villain Era (October 13, 2023)

The concept of the villain era has been dominating social media and our social lives. I have been reminded of the idea that every villain has an origin story that has led to the unlocking of their dark side.

But I believe that not all that is dark is supposed to be wicked and negative. The dark can be deep and disturbing in a positive way. It makes us perceive and recognize our authentic realities so we are able to embrace that part of us and become whole as individuals.

And I know that nobody is alone in this villain era, including me. We can be together in this era of individuality, self-discovery, and personal fulfillment. But because of a toxic Filipino culture that is popularly known as pakikisama, we have ended up thinking that we are all alone in life.

I have known that human beings, like what I am, are social creatures. I, with everybody else, live in the context of sociality that shapes our thoughts and behaviors. And I have come to think that sociality has caused and sustained the culture of pakikisama.

Pakikisama is a Filipino word associated with the concept of social interaction and defined as getting along with others. However, in getting along with others, I have experienced peer pressure.

Peer pressure, for me, is the force I encounter when other people try to influence my thinking and actions, and it can affect me in either a positive or negative way. And it turns out that pakikisama has meant two different things to me.

In my perspective, one meaning of pakikisama is giving in to positive peer pressure. And the other is giving in to negative peer pressure.

When I have given in to positive peer pressure, my sense of individuality is strengthened. I felt happiness and satisfaction being myself because of the people that have brought out the best in me.

Giving in to positive pressure has made me realize that I am a powerhouse that is filled with strengths and skills. Because of the people that have provided me with positive peer pressure, I have gained trust in myself as I maintained harmonious relationships with them.

I have adopted values and beliefs that have morally nourished me. I have participated in the activities that have been making me the best person that I can ever be.

My experience has made me realize that positive peer pressure ought to be upheld in this villain era. Nobody is alone as we ought to give and take positive energies, and grow and learn individually while being each other's support system.

However, as positivity is being brought into my life by positive peer pressure, I am also exposed to negative peer pressure that has been trying to bring negativity into my life.

But I have begun resisting it because it made me lose my sense of individuality. I do not want to find myself in sadness and disappointment again with the people that brought out the worst in me.

By giving in to negative peer pressure before, I thought of myself as a wimp that was filled with weaknesses and incapabilities. I lost trust in myself as I suffered discomforting relationships with negative people.

So I have been preventing myself from giving in to negative peer pressure because I do not want to adopt values and beliefs that once morally destroyed me. I do not want to participate in the activities that used to make me the worst person that I ought not to be.

Thinking about my own experience versus what others are going through, I have come to realize that negative peer pressure may have provoked the rise of the villain era.

So instead of tolerating the toxicity and negativity surrounding the culture of pakikisama, I believe we ought to redefine it as building ourselves and one another through positive peer pressure.

When positive peer pressure is being strengthened and sustained, the villain era can succeed with its purpose for individuality, self-discovery, and personal fulfillment of the greater good.

Peach Fuzz (December 29, 2023)

It was on the 7th day of December 2023 when the Pantone Color Institute, a global leading source of color expertise, proudly revealed the much-awaited Pantone Color of the Year for 2024.

The chosen Pantone Color of the Year 2024 will serve as a reminder that the vital part of life is health, stamina, and strength. It will highlight the importance of the inner selves and human connection along with creativity and respite.

It will focus on wellbeing, warmth, and comfort through tuning into who we are as well as coming together with others. It will reflect our feeling for seemingly simpler days, at the same time will display a more contemporary ambiance, and by its presence will lift us into the future.

As the Pantone Color Institute underwent the color selection process with thoughtful consideration on emotional aspects and global culture, it has finally presented the Pantone Color of the Year 2024 as the PANTONE 13-1023 Peach Fuzz.

PANTONE 13-1023 Peach Fuzz is a velvety gentle peach, an appealing hue between pink and orange. It is a clean tone that carries a vintage vibe yet impacts today's world.

I couldn't help but appreciate and admire it. The PANTONE 13-1023 Peach Fuzz has effortlessly connected with my recent personal narratives, which I assuredly know shall inevitably continue in the approaching new year.

With profound reason and genuine emotion, I have naturally linked the PANTONE 13-1023 Peach Fuzz to my recent three key experiences in life emphasizing the notions of compassion within the spirit, empathy within the community, and kindness within the digital world.

Compassion within the spirit

In January 2023, I shamelessly gained the courage to openly share my life story through a prestigious broadcasting program. I wholeheartedly and mindfully composed my personal narrative and bravely submitted it through their official email address.

The host notified me about her immediate schedule of reading my life story on air. As my initial reaction, I excitedly watched her live on an online platform.

As I anticipatedly witnessed the sharing of my personal narrative through a broadcasting program, I suddenly felt emotional and was strongly overwhelmed by the feeling of release.

For the first time in my life, I was able to wholly accept myself with my own shadows, monsters, and demons. I fearlessly presented my life story, truly turned capable of embracing every part of me, deeply experienced being whole, and wonderfully integrated as a spirit.

Empathy within the community

In September 2023, I cluelessly agreed to meet a stranger from my online literary community. I gradually learned that he was a God-fearing and a true admirer of mine.

He openly and willingly shared his life story with me, and as we equally communicated with each other, we turned out having started a divinely guided connection and developing a real bond.

At first, I found it extremely hard to believe that a person like him physically and spiritually existed. But as I constantly underwent the process of knowing him more, I became fully convinced that he was a God-given gift to me.

I suddenly realized that intentionally living in my light was meant to be perceived by another whom I'm fated to connect with, for our lights to unite and transform into one greater light whose life had been from and of the divine.

Kindness within the digital world

In May 2021, I purposefully started presenting my literary works on an online platform with the aim to bring life to creativity and share insights with others.

By making my poems, essays, and stories visible online, I was able to learn the significance of literature in improving the quality of my life as well as touching the lives of another in a positive way.

As I openly posted my real thoughts and feelings, I found myself interconnected with everyone else, particularly when my online followers extended their appreciation to me.

I really felt my special place in the world every time someone expressed their gratitude for my online messages. I came to realize that kindness would always be a thing to give and take.

Through these recent three key experiences of mine, I can't help but hope for the continuation of compassion, empathy, and kindness in the future.

I deeply wish that the Pantone Color of the Year 2024, PANTONE 13-1023 Peach Fuzz, will bring a sense of self, a sense of community, and a sense of oneness in the new year.

Thoughts to Ponder: Plan B (March 4, 2024)

I happened to watch a TikTok video and heard its speaker say that he does not recommend others to have Plan B because it only sends them to failure.

At first, I was impressed by his viewpoint because it imbues conviction, power, and success. It initially made me think that we have the will to make everything possible, and the way to make things happen.

As he continued, he emphasized the value of consistency rather than Plan B. It is because others decide to give up with the reason that they have another plan. But if they are being consistent, they eventually achieve their primary goals.

I agree with his concept of consistency, due to my belief that we cannot always get what we want on the first try or the first time. I can actually relate to the notion that individuals who did not make it in one take, are never inferior to those who made it as a first timer.

Being repeat takers does not make anyone lesser than any other individuals, because getting it right or passing it in the first attempt is not the only measure of success.

Success is not merely about not experiencing any failure at all, it is about acknowledging the facticity of failure, flipping the next circumstances, and converting them into success.

Exactly like my personal experiences, I had retakes in my life.

When I was in college, I took the Second Level Civil Service Examination, and I failed. But in the second take, I passed the exam and attained professional eligibility.

When I was employed in a government institution, I took a psychological examination, and my intellectual level was below average. But after my retake, the result was superior.

When I took my master's degree comprehensive examinations, out of twelve subjects, I failed in one subject. But when I retook the exam for that one subject, I passed it.

I admit that having consistency has had a huge impact on me as I went through some of my professional life events. But I disagree with the outlook that Plan B means failure.

In my opinion, Plan B as a backup plan is not being conditioned or being programmed to fail. Plan B is about broadening the mindset and recognizing the facticity of the outside forces.

Though we have been trained to trust ourselves or to be self-made individuals, we need the favor of the Higher Being we believe in and the support of the individuals involved in our endeavors.

Nobody is isolated or separated from the rest, what we need is to find the circle where we can grow and learn the most, while acknowledging the fact that basically we are all interconnected. Plan B reminds us that no man is an island.

It is not about being opinionated and ensuring that we are not dictated by others. It is about knowing that we are not the center of all, but we are parts of a whole where we ought to be aligned.

In my opinion, Plan B as an alternative strategy is not assuming or predicting the end as failure. It is about being conscious of the chance to bounce back by turning inward to our purpose.

We cannot always figure things out in the early stages of our lives, as from time to time, we can encounter moments of realization and times of enlightenment.

We need to learn to admit that when our first solution does not work, we have the choice not to stick with it, to come up with a different response induced by the experience.

Plan B reminds us that rough seas make stronger sailors. It is not about being the same person with a strong fearless spirit by denying what is ineffective. It is about being aware of human limits so we can allow our spiritual existence to maneuver us.

In my opinion, Plan B as a fallback, is not expecting defeat all the time or considering ourselves as losers. Instead, it is about being receptive to diversity or randomness of happenings.

We cannot be happy-go-lucky always to the point that we obviously avoid control issues, but we need to understand that we ought to do the work it takes with the faith that the source provides.

Nothing is set in stone and change is the only constant. We ought to accept the reality that what used to be applicable may not be useful anymore, so it helps when we become innovative.

Plan B reminds us that we are beings in process. It is not about preserving our primitive state of thinking by being close-minded towards progress in general. It is about going through the inevitable unfolding of mysteries and insights.

Puzzle Pieces (August 28, 2024)

One Sunday as I was taking my time beholding various artworks exhibited by a prestigious university, one painting really caught my eye.

The painting depicted an image of a person that had a huge puzzle space in her chest. Around her were puzzle pieces scattered about containing different images.

At first, I thought that the artwork implied the tendency of human beings to normally look outside when we feel something has been missing in us. However, as I stared longer at the painting, I noticed that none of the scattered puzzle pieces would fit the space in her chest.

So I thought that the void within could not be filled by external factors, particularly if they were only based on the views of others.

I studied the images contained in the puzzle pieces closer and realized that the artwork could really mean something deeper and more. As I reflected on what the images might signify, I was overwhelmed with insights.

The first puzzle piece contained the image of lungs. Instantly I thought of lungs as the symbol of body, health, and something related to the physical. So I figured it means that we should give attention to our body, because the body had been said to be the temple of God.

I thought that it would be okay to eat well, exercise, and even get enough sunlight.

However, the downside of focusing too much on our body could be purely basing our worth on its size and shape, which commonly results in body shaming. Making our body look healthy isn't all about beauty, but brains as well, because it takes the right information and discipline for our body to look good and become good.

So lungs could mean two different things, in my point of view, particularly the contradicting concepts of beauty and brains.

Next, the second puzzle piece contained the image of a lotus. The first idea that came to my mind was spirituality and sense of self.

Initially I thought that there was nothing wrong with prioritizing our spiritual life because it had been our essence. But I came to realize that we cannot just feed our spirit, we also need to feed our stomach.

So I would say that we should pair our sense of spirituality with a sense of practicality. We ought to couple our sense of self with a sense of survival, as the lotus also signifies survival.

So the image could be interpreted in contrasting ways; it could either be about spirituality or survival.

Then, the third puzzle piece contained the image of a compass. Right away, I was reminded by the idea of direction.

The compass has been a positive symbol because it represents the concept of going places and improving life. It could also mean leadership skills, accumulating wealth, and the possibility of success.

But as I reflected better on the image, I remembered the notion of a moral compass. So the object could not be all about physical movement or tangible measurement. Because moral compass is about our sense of right and wrong, the just and unjust. It highlights the value of relationships.

This image could mean that we could not be all about competition but also cooperation. It could suggest that we ought to compete for one particular role or position, but cooperate with others who rightfully acquired their own positions.

So the compass could be contradictory in meaning, too, because it could be about competition or cooperation.

Finally, the fourth puzzle piece contained the image of a star with a check. My first thought was about popularity that had brought inspiration and influence. Usually, star qualities refer to celebrities.

But the downside of considering popular or public figures as stars is the possibility of becoming delusional and people pleasing. On the other side, we could perceive the star as the sign of our Savior that was born in Bethlehem.

So it depends on us how we would define the star. We could put celebrities on pedestals and consider them the star, or we could humble ourselves before our Savior.

The star could really mean two different things: honor or humility.

Nevertheless, no matter how I view the image, determining what exactly had been the missing puzzle piece in a person would be subjective. We could never really tell what would make someone whole, instead, it's a personal process or internal experience.

It had been and would be different for everyone, so we should let others go through their personal journey. As such, we should also allow ourselves to be subjective in knowing ourselves as we go through our own journey toward the center of our very existence.

Inner Speech (November 27, 2024)

I have resolved to guard my boundaries; I will no longer hesitate to restrict others. I will deny them my access if by doing so, I can restore my peace of mind, sanity, and sense of self and purpose in life.

I don't deserve to be ridiculed and criticized by people who don't have the ability to see through my passion and craft. I will continue to pursue my passion though it means blocking people from it. I need the right circle, not the wrong crowd.

I have been deeply wounded by their judgment, I am even scarred by the bitter memories they leave in me. But I will be patient. I will process the pain as it demands to be felt until it produces a stronger, wiser, and better me.

I have deprived myself of being showy or spontaneous, but it depends on my will and resolve to stop suppressing my emotions. I only hurt myself as I keep hiding in a comfort zone, which is not comfortable at all.

I have extended good deeds to others, but in return, they misuse and badmouth the vulnerability I allow them to see. They take advantage and abuse my kindness, so I have opted to act cold as the pain inside me goes deep, spreads wide, and becomes severe.

I have kept to myself, as I ignore the world around me. I have declined to exert effort and time, and they have made me appear as a bad person. But on my part, I only protect myself against more abuse and toxicity that have been eating my concept and image of myself. They point out what they have labeled as wrong with me, but they never assess what they have been doing to me that has resulted in my silence and coldness.

I have been struggling for a long time, for my interaction with them just keeps on repeating; learning and growth are out of sight. I have become moody and lazy about life in general, as I emotionally create a world of my own to somehow have the prudence to go on with my life.

They may condemn me for being useless and inaccessible, but the truth is by depriving them of the power over me, I gain relief. I have not ever felt guilty when I begin to realize that my being kind doesn't depend on how they agree with my perspective. I am kind when I am kind to myself first, though it means shielding myself from those who dictate, manipulate, and disempower me.

I continue to work on myself, in alignment with what feels right and good for me, not for the sake of their approval. They are not my standard, so I work in my time and pace, not when they are around or right in front of me evaluating my performance based on the criteria they only invent with their biased and lousy stand in life.

I alone have been defending myself, and I have stopped anticipating protection from others. I even have tried to meet halfway or find common ground with them, but they end up badmouthing me. They have made me appear unlovable and irreconcilable, but it is them who deprive love and reconciliation to take place between us. They have destroyed my childhood, but I will never allow them to ruin me further.

I am worthy of love and all the good things that come along with it. The right person will see through me and all the things I have been through and will help me heal and start anew. So I will protect that person, and make him understand that the people who have conditioned me are not his obligation. The love we have is what matters, and it doesn't involve anybody else.

We will allow God to be the center of our relationship, and not other people who have rationalized the existence of the Supreme Being, and assume that they are responsible for us two. I am his Godsend as he is to me, so we will protect each other, though it means against the people around us.

So I choose to go where the love, grace, and power of the Supreme Being flows, and be the living testimony of His goodness.

About the Author

Ancel Mondia

Ancel Mondia is an Ilongga NBDB-registered author/writer, the Fiction - Woman Writer of the Year 2023 by Ukiyoto Publishing, and a graduate of Master of Arts in English and Literature.

9 789367 955017